IN LOVING MEMORY OF

VERENA MALLORY

FROM HER FAMILY

No-Name Baby

NANCY BO FLOOD

namelos
South Hampton, New Hampshire

Library of Congress Control Number: xxxxxx

ISBN 978-1-60898-117-5 (hardcover : alk. paper)
ISBN 978-1-60898-118-2 (pbk. : alk. paper)
ISBN 978-1-60898-119-9 (ebk.)

namelos
www.namelos.com

To my mother, Shirley Mae Bergera Bohac,
and to my grandmother, Elizabeth "Bessie" Tryner,
who sang to the baby in the box

Contents

Flat Gray Stones

Sophie pressed her thumbs against the cold glass, melting two small circles through the frost. She scratched along the icy edges until there was a clear space wide enough to peer through. The window looked out across the farmyard, past the broad front of the red barn with its dark roof sitting solid and snug like a winter hat.

She looked past the pig sty. The old sows were already pushing at each other, fighting over food scraps.

Her gaze paused at the chicken coop, which leaned against one side of the barn as if holding on. Then she looked out to the orchard.

Sophie shivered. She remembered last night's dream and the gray stones—a whole row of them like the ones under the trees. Each stone was etched with letters that she couldn't quite read.

Sophie squinted, trying to see all the way to the fence that bordered the cornfield. Maybe Karl was there waiting. Maybe.

She pulled the warm wool shawl tight around her shoulders.

A Bucket of Slops

"Sophie! What's keeping you?" Mama called. "I can hear you tiptoeing around up there. Chores won't wait forever."

"I'm coming, I'm coming!" Sophie frowned, still thinking about the dream. Maybe Nonna was right—maybe Mama having this baby was too dangerous. But Mama was set on trying. Two more months; then everything would be all right. Everyone would be fine. Sophie took a deep breath, glanced at her reflection in the mirror, wiped a bit of frost off her forehead, and headed downstairs.

She stopped at the bottom step and looked around the kitchen. Aunt Rae wasn't up yet, thank goodness. Having her aunt arrive unannounced on the train from Chicago hadn't helped calm anyone's nerves. She and Aunt Rae had always been bristly, but this week they had hardly exchanged a civil word.

Without so much as a "good morning," Mama held out the bucket.

"Oh, please, not again," Sophie pleaded. "I've been hauling the slops every morning this week." One look in that bucket and her empty stomach lurched. Globs of pork grease floated in curdled milk between blackened potato peels. "Don't make me feed those stinky pigs again, Mama. You know they give me the willies." A thought came to her, and her dark eyes sparkled with a bit of mischief. "Maybe Aunt Rae would enjoy taking some morning breakfast to the pigs."

Her mother set the bucket down and crossed her arms, resting them on her huge belly, the belly everyone was worrying about. Mama's legs were swollen and her thin face was pale. Just seven more weeks till June. Then this baby could be born strong and healthy, instead of coming too early like the others.

"Tell you what, Sophie," Mama said, more gently this time. "I'll slop the pigs. You pick the eggs."

Which was exactly what Sophie had hoped for.

"The fresh air will do me some good." Mama paused, then smiled. "You might want to take the last of the cake with you. Papa and Karl will be getting ready to plow. That young man just might appreciate a piece of your good chocolate cake. I suspect you were thinking of stopping by anyway."

Sophie smiled back, trying to ignore the warm blush creeping up her neck.

"But don't dally too long. Your Aunt Rae needs your help here at the house"—Mama paused, looked at Sophie—"and we don't want her getting upset."

"Thanks, Mama."

Sophie picked up the cake, slipped out the door, and hurried right past the chicken coop and through the orchard until she reached the fence along the upper field.

Papa and Karl were already at the tractor, adjusting the plow. Sophie handed the cake to Karl. "Mama said to bring it down."

"That's mighty thoughtful of your ma. Please give her my thanks." Karl smiled and tipped his hat. "And I thank you for bringing it."

"I hope you enjoy it." Sophie could feel her face heating up again. She returned his nod, then hurried back toward the chicken coop. She paid no attention to the soft clucking of the hens as she slipped her hand under their scratchy feathers, her fingers feeling for eggs. She was thinking about Karl, the way he looked at her and smiled when he thanked her for the cake.

Now she had to hurry and get back to the house. She had an apron of eggs to carry to the kitchen before Aunt Rae started asking why she'd been gone so long.

The dirt path through the orchard ended at the top of the hill where their farmhouse stood, square, white, two-story, solid. Sophie kicked through the puddles, cracking the thin layers of ice, careful not to let any eggs fall. Mama always told her to take a basket along when gathering eggs, but Sophie liked the nest her apron made with the sides held up—a nest of beautiful eggs, each a different shade of brown. Smooth and warm.

Sophie paused for a moment. She heard the pigs snorting and squealing, their grunts getting louder. She looked across the farmyard at the pig sty. Mama had the slop bucket propped on the upper rail.

Mama lifted the pail up a bit higher, high enough so the slop could pour over the fence into the feed trough. Mama strained as she lifted the pail with both hands. But then Mama's feet began to slip. They slipped right out from under her.

Mama was falling!

Sophie reached out. She tried to reach clear across the barnyard to stop the falling.

"Mama!"

The eggs slipped out of her apron. Orange yolk splattered across the black mud.

The slop bucket crashed down. It clanged and rattled as it rolled past the pig pen, clanged and rattled until it hit the barn. *Bang.*

Mama lay curled up tight. She lay there in the mud, quiet. And then she began making soft moaning sounds.

Moaning sounds she was still making when Papa carried her up to the house.

Birth

In the back corner of the kitchen Sophie sat still and alone, afraid to leave, afraid that something more would happen unless she was there to stop it. Her eyes scanned the kitchen as if it were unfamiliar, taking in every detail. Was there a clue somewhere, a hint about what she needed to do so that her mother would be fine, so that this baby would be fine?

She looked across the room. Aunt Rae, her mother's older sister, was staring at her, then looked away. Her face was drawn, her jaw set tight, her lips shut in a straight, hard line. Aunt Rae was a mystery. She didn't talk much, and what she did say was often short and terse, as if she had only a small pocket of precious words that needed to last a long time.

Silence filled the room like an uninvited guest. Every little sound broke the quiet. Even the tick, tick, ticking of the clock felt like an endless scolding. That clock had been a wedding gift from Italy that Papa had given Mama long ago.

Fire in the woodstove crackled. Water in the teakettle hissed. Steam popped and pinged, skittering across the hot iron stove. And sometimes, from upstairs, up in Mama and Papa's room, there were footsteps, moans. And then a stream of

Italian, Nonna's voice. Words that Sophie couldn't understand. Outside on the porch, Papa chopped wood. *Whack. Tumble-clunk.* But the wood box was full. *Whack. Tumble-clunk.*

Aunt Rae pushed a wisp of hair back into her tight bun and poked it with a pin. That curl would cause no more trouble. "Too early. Again, too early." She sat straight-backed at the round oak table, folding and refolding freshly laundered cloths.

After a while Aunt Rae spoke again, to no one in particular. "Life's not fair," she said. "Never was." Her voice was as sharp and sour as her words. "I don't know why she wanted to have this baby." She looked at Sophie as if wanting to say more, but just shook her head.

Aunt Rae was older than Mama by five years. The two were so different. Anna, Sophie's mother, was short and slender with golden hair and sky-blue eyes that usually sparkled with an easy happiness. Aunt Rae had taken all the darkness in the family, thick black hair and deep brown eyes and a face that seldom smiled. She hardly ever visited, and when she did, she never stayed long. Even then she mostly kept to herself in the parlor, playing song after song on the big old piano. No one ever said it out loud, but they all were relieved when Aunt Rae went home to Chicago.

"Too many weeks early. Too many." Aunt Rae's hands never stopped moving, never stopped folding or rearranging the cloths from one stack to another.

Sophie stared at her.

Aunt Rae looked up, tilted her head, and seemed surprised to see her niece sitting there. "Better get some rest," she said, frowning. "Nothing more for us to do tonight. Nonna is a good midwife. The best."

"Not yet ..."

"Sophia Rosa! Go to bed." Aunt Rae's words ran right over Sophie's.

"I'm old enough to wait up! I'm nearly fourteen, and I—"

"I know perfectly well how old you are, young lady. It's time for you to be in bed."

The clock kept ticking, ticking.

Aunt Rae spread her hands across her lap. "Sophie, please. Everyone's help will be needed when this baby is born."

Sophie didn't answer. She was determined to stay where she was until she knew that her mother was all right. She ached to be near Mama, to see her or even just hear her voice. She loved listening to Mama talk when they worked together, stringing beans or wringing out the wash. Mama would tell story after story about all the funny things she and Rae had done growing up together on the farm. What would it be like to have a sister, someone to share secrets while hiding in the hayloft or racing like wild horses across the fields?

The kitchen door banged open. Papa backed in, hunched over, carrying an armload of wood. The cold night air came blowing in right with him. Sophie hurried over and pushed the door shut, then starting stacking the split logs Papa had dumped in front of the wood bin.

Papa didn't take any notice, didn't look at anyone. He warmed his hands, red and chapped, over the stove, his eyes fixed on the stairs. Aunt Rae handed him a cup of steaming coffee. Nobody said a word.

Papa took a big gulp, set the cup on the table, turned, and left as quick as he had come in. Once again Sophie heard the sound of his boots as he clumped across the porch, the axe splitting cold wood. *Whack. Tumble-clunk.*

Aunt Rae glared at the clock. "Way past midnight. Get some rest, Sophie."

"Did it take this long when I was born?"

"Sophie, please, no questions. Not tonight." Aunt Rae reached for the stack of cloths.

"Let me help."

"No!" her aunt snapped.

A loud moan came from upstairs. Then another. Papa flung open the door, his eyes wide. Aunt Rae crossed herself, murmuring, "Jesus, Mary, and Joseph have mercy."

A long, awful cry. A scream.

Papa bolted up the stairs. Aunt Rae was right behind.

Sophie couldn't move.

Another terrible cry. Mama's cry.

A Too-Early Baby

The cries stopped. Sophie's ears hurt from trying to hear *something*. She knew babies are supposed to cry when they're born.

Jesus, Mary, and Joseph, let Mama be all right. Please let Mama's baby live.

Finally footsteps, then voices. Sophie looked up. Aunt Rae stood at the top of the stairs. Sophie could not see her clearly, only that she held on to the railing with one hand and with the other she held a large metal pail.

"The birthing is done."

Sophie opened her mouth but could not make any words come out. Her throat was tight. Her hands were trembling.

Aunt Rae came down the stairs, step by step. She set down the pail, smoothed back Sophie's hair, and said softly, "You have a baby brother, Sophie."

The gentleness in her aunt's voice surprised Sophie. "But Mama?"

"Your mother's tired, plumb worn out."

"But she's all right?"

Aunt Rae nodded.

"I want to see her." Sophie started up the stairs.

Aunt Rae stepped in front of Sophie, blocking her way. Her voice was quiet but stern. "Not now, Sophie. Not now. Your mother's resting ... finally." Rae picked up the pail and looked directly at Sophie. "Let your mother rest."

"I won't upset her, just hold her hand a minute, only for a minute." Sophie's words came out too loud, too shrill, but she had to get upstairs. She needed to tell Mama how sorry she was, that she'd been stupid and selfish and that she wouldn't complain about the pigs again, not ever again. "I won't cry and upset her."

"If you want to help your mother, let her be. Let her rest."

Sophie looked up the stairs and clenched her fists. Her aunt was right. She turned around and reached toward the pail, about to say *Let me help with that*, but pulled her hand away. The pail was filled with blood-soaked towels.

Her aunt lugged the pail to the sink, dumped everything out, and began rinsing the towels.

"How can I help?"

Aunt Rae picked up a towel and twisted it hard but didn't answer.

"You'll tell me when Mama wakes up?"

"Sophie, please."

"I need to see Mama."

"Nonna will stay with her and the baby. There is nothing more anyone can do right now. If you don't get some rest you won't be any help to anyone."

Sophie backed away, pushed open the kitchen door, and stumbled to the edge of the porch. She grabbed hold of the railing, squeezed to fight back tears. She filled her lungs with deep, slow breaths. The air was cold. She stared out across the fields, looked toward the eastern horizon.

Morning was beginning to brighten the rim of sky above the cornfields, just as it did yesterday and would again tomorrow. Mama needed rest, that was all. Aunt Rae said so. Sophie stared at the wide rolling fields, the newly plowed earth, black as coal. Those long orderly rows, one beside another, straight and familiar, glistened in the morning light. Life was as it should be. Blackbirds and a few robins fluttered low over the furrows, searching for worms.

The baby was just a little early. Mama ... she would rest. Rest and be fine. Sophie and Aunt Rae could do the household chores. Karl was helping Papa with the spring plowing. *Karl said he would wait by the orchard when the day's plowing was done.* Her stomach lurched a little. *That was already yesterday.*

Bantam roosters began their cockadoodling, aiming to out-crow each other. A new morning. The day was coming alive.

Sophie closed her eyes and went way inside herself, so that God, wherever he was, would know she meant every word.

Let Mama live. If you need to take someone, take me. That would be fair.

A cold breeze blew through Sophie's thin shawl. Gray

clouds piled up along the east, dimming the thin line of sun-light. Sophie shivered; she should have put on a coat.

"Sophie!" someone called from inside.

Sophie opened the kitchen the door. Aunt Rae was still standing by the sink.

Her face was red and puffy, and tears filled her eyes. Sophie stared. Aunt Rae never cried. Never.

Aunt Rae looked at Sophie. "It's all right, Sophie, this time it's all right." She nodded toward the stairs. "Nonna is calling you."

Olive Oil and a Box

Nonna came down the stairs one careful step at a time. Her arms cradled a small bundle next to her bosom. Her strong, weathered hands pressed against the soft white wrapping.

Nonna straightened her back, smiled, and rattled off a stream of Italian. Aunt Rae rushed to the pantry. Nonna switched to carefully pronounced English. "We have a baby, this beautiful little angel."

Sophie didn't move. Nonna was smiling—a real smile. Her many laugh wrinkles creased around her eyes and mouth.

"Mama?" Sophie asked.

"*Sì, sì*, your mama is good, *sta bene*. Your papa watches while she rests. Now—this is our work. This *bambino. Adesso, subito!*" Nonna's words sang out.

Sophie came alive. Aunt Rae was still in the pantry searching for something. Pans were clanking, glass jars jingling.

Sophie poked her head in. "What are you looking for? What does Nonna want?"

Aunt Rae held up an amber glass bottle. "This! The olive oil Uncle Frank sent. I found it!"

"Olive oil?"

"*Sì, sì*," Nonna called from the kitchen, "oil from Tuscany. *Il migliore*, the finest! *Sì*, rich with life." She waved toward the stove. "Regina Maria, the iron skillet."

Regina Maria. Nonna called Aunt Rae by her full name only when she was upset or had something important to say.

Aunt Rae reached for the large frying pan.

"No, *la padellina,* the little one. Warm it. *Presto!* Pour in the oil. Ah, *sì*, warm oil from olives, *dolce come un bacio,* sweet as a kiss. *Brava.*"

Nonna stopped, turned. She looked around the kitchen, *her* kitchen. She was the queen of every inch.

"Sophia! Here, come here."

Sophie hesitated. "Me?"

"*Sì.*" Her grandmother's voice was serious. Usually Nonna was pointing and talking, sometimes hugging and even singing while giving commands, but not this morning. Nonna spoke quickly, words spilling out. "This beautiful little angel … *bellissimo angioletto.* We must warm him."

The skillet was on the stove. Aunt Rae poured in the oil.

Sophie had to ask again. "Is Mama really all right?"

"*Sì*, your Mama is resting, *bene. We* do not rest, we take care of *bambino. Subito*, scrub your hands. Be ready!"

Sophie washed and dried her hands quickly.

Nonna motioned. "*Vieni*! Come closer."

Sophie's eyes widened.

"*Sì, sì.* You are the sister. Now you help your brother."

Sophie glanced at her aunt.

"Do what Nonna tells you," Aunt Rae said. "Remember, last summer, how she saved those Bertolli twins? She has a special way with babies." Aunt Rae tried to smile. "Yes ... and with mothers."

With Nonna there was no arguing; not even Mama could out-argue her. Nonna had wanted Mama to have this baby at the new hospital in Joliet because, as she explained to Papa, her hands waving and her words determined, "This is a *new* country and a *new* century. We are new—shiny new—Americans!"

Mama didn't want to go to a hospital, even a new one. The way things turned out, Mama got her way.

Nonna dipped her fingers in the warm oil and tested the temperature against her wrist, then shooed Aunt Rae away with a wave of her hand. She turned to Sophie. "Now we care for this little brother."

Nonna cradled the bundle of baby with one arm and crossed herself with the other, her lips whispering a quick prayer. Then she set the baby in the middle of the pile of blankets warming on the stove.

Sophie leaned closer. Somewhere in there was her brother, but swaddled up so tight that only the very top of his head stuck out.

"Warm, always to be warm, this our baby needs, like a newly hatched chick. Our *bambino*, a tiny chick, no feathers, no fat." Nonna nodded. "Warm, *sì*, we will keep you warm, little angel. And this, *olio d'oliva*."

"Olive oil, Nonna?"

"*Sì*, you will learn. Oil gives life."

Nonna gazed at the baby for a moment. Then with one hand she cradled the baby's head, and with the other she gently unwound the swaddling cloth as if unwrapping Mama's hand-blown wedding crystal.

"More oil, Sophia. Pour into the pan. One knuckle deep. *Perfetto.* With oil, with warmth, we soothe this baby, so gentle, everywhere, little fingers, legs, tiny toes, and very much his tummy and chest."

"With olive oil?"

"*Sì*, we rub in life, calling, calling."

Nonna held the tiny face close to hers, almost nose to nose. She whispered words in Italian, then kissed his eyes and his wrinkled little forehead. "Be strong, *angelino*, precious angel. Be strong."

Nonna steadied his head with one hand as she pressed his curled-up arms and legs to his chest. "All tucked back together," she explained. "Now he feels safe. Soon he becomes calm."

When she slipped her hand out from behind his head, he frowned, his little lips quivering, and then cried. Like a kitten. A soft sound, high and scared.

Such a tiny bit of life! Sophie saw that this entire baby, her brother, could fit in the cradle of Nonna's hand. He fought for each breath, his chest caving in and nearly collapsing with the effort, his face turning dusky, blue-tinged. His skin was mottled, covered with a white waxy coating streaked red with blood. Sophie stared at the stub of shiny blue cord that marked the place for his bellybutton. Her head felt light, the kitchen felt closed in, hot and stuffy.

Nonna glanced at her granddaughter. "*Dio mio!* Sit down. Sit! Head on the table. Breathe slow, good."

The baby whimpered, again like a kitten crying.

Nonna whispered soft words. "No crying, little *bambino*, no crying. Breathe, *respira. Va bene*, good. Soon it becomes easy."

Sophie stood back up, her head now clear. She stared at the baby. How tiny and bony, and so fragile. *Live, little brother, live. Mama needs you.*

"Our work begins," Nonna said firmly, as if she had read Sophie's mind. Then she spoke directly to the baby as if giving him orders as well. "*Gallino bambino*, little bantam rooster. Breathe and live. Your mama loves you. Be strong. Your sister, she will love you soon, very soon." She looked at Sophie. "Warm cloths, Sophia, *presto.*"

Nonna dipped the cloth in the warm oil and began massaging. With ever-widening circles she rubbed until the baby's skin pinked up, was less blue and dusky. The baby's grimace relaxed. His breathing slowed, became regular, not so desperate.

Nonna gently swaddled the baby again, and then she dipped two fingers in the kettle's warm water, made the sign of the cross on the baby's forehead, and baptized him.

Antonio Alessandro Giuseppe. Little Tony, live!

Just like that, Nonna baptized a scrawny baby, his skin glistening with oil as he rested in a warm blanket nest.

"If the angels call him"—she quickly made the sign of the cross on her heart—"he is ready. But no worries. Antonio Alessandro, little Tony. Strong *bambino, sì.*" She looked at Sophie and gave another order. "*Subito*, a box."

Sophie didn't understand.

"*Per favore*, a box. We must have a box." Nonna waved toward the cellar stairs. "A box!"

Sophie ran, two stairs at a time, down to the cellar. She knew just where to look. She rushed back up the stairs and then held out the dusty wooden box to Nonna.

"*Brava!* Did you clean it?"

Sophie hadn't had time to take out the garlic heads still in the bottom. It was Papa's prize garlic that he was saving for planting in the fall.

Nonna laughed and dumped the garlic out. "No baby should smell of garlic. Even this *bambino*. Sweet Mary, mother of us all, help our little angel be strong." She set the box down and beckoned to Sophie. "Now, come close."

And then another surprise—Nonna began singing. Sophie did not understand the words, but the melody was from one of Nonna's favorite operas, the one she listened to again and again on the Victrola. As she sang, the soft Italian words flowed like a soothing caress. Everything would be all right. Everything.

"Sing, Sophia."

"Sing? Me, Nonna?"

"Sing to his soul. Ask him to stay."

"I don't know any songs for a baby."

"It doesn't matter. Look into his eyes and sing."

Sophie tried. The baby wasn't as scary-looking now that he wasn't blue and gasping for each breath.

"Sing. He must hear your voice."

Sophie tried. She remembered her grandmother's words: "*Gallino bambino*, little bantam rooster. Little Tony. Breathe and live. Your mama loves you. *Viva, viva.*"

She sang to her brother. The baby opened his eyes and looked right back at her. With wide-open eyes, he stared and stared. Sophie couldn't help but stare right back.

"That's what babies do, Sophia, my little Sophia. After they are born, they look until they find someone, and then they see into your soul. A soul who will love them."

His eyes were wide and dark, and he kept staring and staring as if he really were looking deep into her.

Nonna gently uncurled the baby's fingers, then placed Sophie's finger across his palm. The tiny fingers curled around hers. Curled tight and held on.

Hold on, little brother. Mama needs you.

Nonna crossed herself and closed her eyes. She whispered words of thanks. "*Brava.* Now open the oven, Sophia. It is warm? Not hot? No cooking Antonio. *Sì*, you hear that, our *bambino*? *Viva!*" Nonna laughed.

Nonna swaddled Antonio once more, but this time she made the blanket cocoon a little looser around him.

She crossed herself again. *Grazie a Dio*, thanks be to God.

She slipped the baby, box and all, into the oven.

Uninvited

Nonna slapped the sides of her apron. *"Fatta."* She raised her eyebrows, smiled at Sophie. "The baby heard you. He will stay."

Sophie looked down, a little embarrassed, then glanced upstairs.

Nonna followed her gaze. *"Sì.* Sit down. First I will go to the parlor. I must write Antonio's name in the Bible—"

"Now?" Aunt Rae interrupted.

"Sì. He is born. He lives. He is part of our family."

Sophie knew that Nonna kept a record of their family's history, each birth, each death, but she had never seen it. The Bible was kept locked in the parlor cabinet, and the parlor door was kept closed except for funerals, Christmas, Easter, or when Aunt Rae was playing the piano.

"Can I watch?" Sophie asked.

Nonna looked at Aunt Rae, then shook her head. "Not now, Sophie. If Rae is needed upstairs, someone must be right here by the baby. Your papa is upstairs, but what do men know?" She waved her hands as if dismissing the whole notion of men. "They know cows and tractors, but about women and babies? Nothing."

Sophie smiled at her grandmother. When Nonna was near, talking, cooking, her hands always busy, the world felt right, everything as it should be.

Nonna stepped toward the parlor, then paused to peek into the warming oven. She stared and stared.

Sophie's heart started racing. "Is something wrong?"

"Nothing, nothing. Just so beautiful." She crossed herself one more time, opened the parlor door, and hurried in.

Papa stood at the top of the stairs, cleared his throat. Sophie looked up. Her aunt did too.

"A problem?" Aunt Rae asked, frowning.

"Anna is sleeping now, but she was asking for tea. That's good, isn't it?"

Poor Papa—he looked befuddled. In the barn he was calm, always confident about how to fix whatever was wrong with an animal or an engine.

Aunt Rae placed one finger across her lips and with her other hand signaled him to come down quietly. She began pumping the sink handle and ticking off orders. "I'll make tea. When Nonna comes back, I'll go up and stay with Anna. Soon as the water's boiling, I'll—"

There was a soft knock on the kitchen door.

Aunt Rae clanged the kettle onto the stove and looked at the door disapprovingly. "Who on earth could that be?"

Papa glanced at Sophie. "Sounds like someone's paying us a call. You ladies take care of our visitor. I'll get back upstairs with Anna."

"As if we don't have enough on our minds!" Aunt Rae marched to the door and pulled it open.

"Hello, ah, Miss ..."

"Miss Rossini," Aunt Rae said.

Karl stood awkwardly in the doorway, hunched over with his arms full. He tried to take off his hat, a brown tweed cap, but nearly dropped what he was holding, so he just gave a little bow. "My mother sends her greetings and this pot of soup and, ah ..." He was still talking to Aunt Rae, but his eyes glanced around the room until he saw Sophie. "And fresh bread. Rye with caraway. My ma's best. Just baked this morning."

"Karl! How thoughtful." The words popped out of Sophie's mouth before she could stop them. Her hands flew up to her neck; she was already blushing.

Just then Nonna stepped back into the kitchen and saw Karl. "Wonderful! Soup and bread, sì."

Karl was still in the doorway, unsure of what to do with the round iron pot and the large loaf of bread balanced on top. The yeasty aroma was already drifting into the kitchen.

"Stay right there." Aunt Rae scowled as she took the soup and bread from Karl and put them on a small table near the door. "No need to be traipsing in here with muddy boots this hour of the morning."

Nonna shot her a disapproving glance. "Regina Maria! Such manners! This young man is a classmate of Sophie's."

Aunt Rae glared back.

Nonna tilted her head toward Sophie, indicating with a wave of her open hand that she should say something.

Sophie blushed even deeper. "We thank you kindly, but—" It was hard to get the words out. She swallowed. "How did you know? I mean, about my mother?"

"Sophia!" Aunt Rae glowered at her.

"Your father, I mean, Mr. Berta, ah, he said, that is, he asked if I would finish the plowing, then he rushed up here— sort of a family emergency, he said, and what I—"

"That's quite enough, young man. I'm sure you are needed back home."

"Of course, yes, I'll be leaving."

Sophie slipped past her aunt. "We do thank you and your family."

"Want me to get your books from school? I figured you might be needed here these next few days."

"Not at all necessary, young man. Our family takes care of family." Aunt Rae took hold of the door. "Give your mother our regards." She paused half a second for Karl to step back, and then she shut the door.

"Such manners! From my own daughter." Nonna threw up her hands and imitated Aunt Rae's scowling face. She lifted the lid off the soup. "Garlic!" Nonna breathed in and smiled. "*Perfetto*. Good for the new mama."

Aunt Rae turned to Sophie. "Who is this boy?"

"He lives nearby. Papa hired him to help afternoons with the plowing. He's a hard worker, Papa says, and smart."

"He knows you?"

"From school. Besides, they're our neighbors, even if their farm is a mile away."

"Neighbors? What's his last name?"

"Kowalski. Karl Kowalski."

"Polish. I should have known. What does his family do?"

"They're from Bohemia, not Poland," Sophie said, correcting her aunt. "They came to this country before the war. They moved to the farm nearby last summer. Karl's family farms, like us."

"Not at all like us. What farm?"

"Two farms down."

"The old Taylor place? Then they rent. Old Man Taylor still owns that farm."

"Karl's father used to work in the coal mines, but that was before the war." Sophie hesitated. "After the war, the mine wouldn't hire him back."

"The war?" Aunt Rae's voice softened. "Was something wrong?"

"He lost an arm."

"Karl's father? He was injured in the war?" Aunt Rae stepped back, and her eyes darted around the room as if searching for something. "Water's boiling. Your mother will be asking for tea I'll bring this up." She took the kettle and hurried upstairs.

"Life, always surprises!" Nonna turned to Sophie, eyebrows raised with an amused look. "You and Karl are classmates, *sì*, but perhaps also something more, good friends?"

"Friends? Sort of, yes, but Karl's a couple of years older than me." Sophie tried to sound very matter-of-fact. She moved the bread and soup to the back of the stove. "Karl's started talking about leaving school. To get a full-time job, not just plowing in the afternoons, even though he has only one more year till graduation. It's hard for his family with his father not being able to work."

Silence settled in the room.

"A nice young man, *sì*?" Nonna's eyes held a twinkle. "Even if he doesn't come from Italy."

Sophie blushed again.

"Oh, the baby! *Gesù Cristo!*" Nonna whipped around and peered into the warming oven. "*Bene, bene*, Sweet Mary, yes, he is breathing fine, soon we begin boiling bottles for water. Babies must drink."

Papa came down the stairs. "Anna is still sleeping. She looks better. Rae told me all about our visitor." He smiled at Sophie. "I heard quite an earful."

Nonna and Sophie exchanged glances.

"Nonna, you need to rest too," Papa said. "Here, sit down. Rae is with Anna. Sophie and I can watch the baby."

"*Sì*," Nonna agreed. "I am tired, I will rest." Nonna sat down with a long sigh in the big oak rocker in the corner of the kitchen. It was her favorite place to sit, since she could keep on eye on everything.

Sophie looked at her papa. "Can I get you some coffee?"

"Sounds good." Papa pulled out two kitchen chairs and set them next to the stove. "You sit too, rest a spell."

Sophie filled Papa's coffee mug. "What did Aunt Rae say about Karl? Why was she so rude?"

Papa leaned back in the chair and rubbed his forehead. "Your Aunt Rae's a complicated woman, Sophie. She's got her reasons for most everything she does. Sometimes it's hard to figure them out."

"She had no reason to be just plain rude."

"Sometimes we are a little hasty in our judgments." He looked again at Nonna. "Maybe your grandma would like some of this good hot coffee."

"Oh, I'm sorry, Nonna," Sophie said.

She poured a cup of strong black coffee into her grandmother's favorite white porcelain cup, then added a dollop of thick cream plus a heaping spoonful of sugar. She took the cup to Nonna, who took a long, slow sip, smiled, and patted Sophie's arm. "Thank you, Sophia."

Sophie waited as her grandmother enjoyed another few swallows and then asked, "Can I go see Mama now?"

Nonna squeezed Sophie's hand. "Soon, Sophia, soon. Anna needs rest."

Nonna drank the last of her coffee, set the cup down, and leaned her head against the curved back of the rocker, her eyes closed. She slipped out her rosary from her apron pocket and held it between her thumb and fingers. Her lips moved soundlessly. Soon the rocking slowed, then stopped. Her breathing deepened and relaxed until she was softly snoring.

Sophie sat down. Her grandmother looked so worn out and tired, even more tired than during the busiest days of August when they all worked from sunup to sundown gathering beets, peas, corn, tomatoes, and every color of beans. They picked, chopped, scalded, and filled quart after quart until rows and rows of canning jars filled the shelves in the cellar.

Now the clock chimed ten—midmorning. Nonna stirred, looked up, and frowned at the clock. She yawned, stood up, shuffled to the warming oven, peered in. "Good. Now I must check the mama."

"I can do that, Nonna. I'll let you know if Mama needs anything."

"No, Sophia, you stay here with the baby." Nonna took off her apron and slowly climbed the stairs.

Sophie looked over at her father. He was sleeping, his mouth slightly open, his chin on his chest. Her own eyes felt heavy and so tired. Maybe she would close them just for a moment. She didn't mean to fall asleep.

"Towels! Bring the hot towels! *Subito*, hurry!"

Sophie's eyes popped open. The clock's hands showed almost eleven.

Footsteps rushed along the upstairs hall.

She looked around the room, confused.

Another shout from upstairs. "*Dio mio!* More towels, *subito!*"

Papa sat upright. "What's going on?"

Rae practically flew down the stairs and stormed straight to the pantry. "More cloths! She's bleeding." She glanced at Sophie, looked at Papa. "Get the doctor, he should be back in town, and ..."—she shook her head, looked away—"the priest."

"God Almighty!" Papa grabbed his hat by the door. "Those roads are nothing but mud." He pulled on his coat and rushed out the door.

Aunt Rae snatched more towels, shoved them under one arm, reached for a pail, and filled it with hot water from the stove.

"Here, let me help." Sophie reached for the handle. Aunt Rae pushed her away.

"You stay here. Watch the baby."

"Let me carry the towels."

"Stay right here."

Outside, the Model T revved up and then roared down the drive, gravel pinging against the fence.

"Mama needs me!"

"No, stay here!"

Sophie grabbed for the bucket. Hot water splashed up, spilled across the floor.

"Now see what you've done. Why can't you do what you're told and stay out of the way!"

Rage and hurt swept through Sophie. She turned, stumbled toward the kitchen door, pushed it open, and fled.

All Things Lost

Sophie ran, not knowing where, away from the house, away from her aunt's accusing voice. She glanced back and stood for a moment trying to stop her trembling and her tears. Then she turned and ran again, past the chickens that had gathered around her, cackling and clucking, waiting for feed she might toss. She got to the corral and stopped. Cows pushed in tightly together in front of the closed barn door, a black-and-white huddle of mooing hungry animals, complaining that milking time was way overdue.

"Papa forgot all about you," Sophie told them. She could not recall a time when Papa had been late milking the cows.

Sophie's favorite cow, Little Bossie, came over to the fence, her calf trailing close behind. Bossie stuck her wide nose over the top rail. Sophie remembered helping Papa pull out Bossie's calf. It seemed like such a long time ago, but it was only a few months back. The calf was big for a first one and stayed stuck too long. Papa reached way up inside Bossie, explaining between breaths how the front hooves needed to be straightened until they were next to the calf's jaw. With the next hard contraction, he pulled until the calf's nose could be seen between two sharp hooves. One more long contraction and the rest of the calf slipped out. Papa and Sophie rubbed the calf's sides, fast and hard, coaxing it to breathe.

Papa had urged, "Come on, little feller. Breathe! Live!"

Mama, you live too.

Once the calf was breathing on its own, Bossie had nudged it until it stood up on its wobbly legs. Sophie and Papa sat on a bale of hay and watched it nose around for Bossie's udders.

Papa had started talking. "Spring is coming, can you feel it? Winter will begin giving way, once again, one more time, Sophie."

It had startled Sophie to hear Papa say her name out loud right there in the barn with nothing but cows and the deep quiet of night. The barn was his place. Mostly he worked in silence. She liked it when she could hear the faint sound of his whistling as he worked.

"Breathe deep and smell it. The earth coming alive. Nothing like it."

Sophie hadn't been sure if Papa was speaking to her or the cows or just letting his thoughts roll around in the cold quiet.

"What a night. Just look at those stars. That Big Dipper ready to pour out water for spring planting. And Orion, standing so big and mighty—imagine all the heartaches and foolishness he's watched. Stars shining for anyone who stops to take a look, reminding us of some greatness we can't understand. A night so pretty as this is a night for being born, Sophie. I hope Anna's baby has a night like this when he decides to show himself. That would make your mother mighty happy."

Now, as Sophie stood on the bottom railing of the corral, she buried her face in the warmth of Bossie's thick coat and wrapped her arms around the animal's huge neck.

Mama, be strong. Dear God, please let my mama live. There can't be any harm in that.

The cows shifted, pushed against one another, mooed louder and looked at Sophie, their big eyes dark and liquid, their wide wet noses breathing out puffs of frosty steam. They stared as if expecting her to push open the door, stand aside so they could file in, same as usual, one at a time, straight to their milking stalls, knowing someone would slide the wooden neck slats shut, give them a rub on the head or a pat on the neck while they chewed the sweet grain.

"Papa's not here," Sophie whispered. "Something terrible is happening. Mama might die and it's all my fault." She walked away, eyes all blurry, and then she heard the hogs snorting and rooting in the mud, fighting over scraps of nothing.

She saw the eggs falling, yoke dripping off frozen clods of black mud.

"You stupid selfish pigs. I hate you!"

It was hard to breathe, to think. She had to get away. She pushed open the side door of the barn and slid through. The sweet smell of last summer's hay wrapped around her. Hand over hand, she climbed the short wooden slats that made a ladder up the barn's back wall and then hoisted herself through the square opening into the hayloft. Her place.

She lay down in the loose hay, waited for her heart to stop racing and the choking in her throat to ease, then stared at the faraway ceiling. Mourning doves roosting on the overhead crossbeams cooed and preened before settling back into sleepy gray shapes. Black-eyed swallows peered from mud nests tucked under the eaves. Sophie curled up tight, breathed in the barn smells—cows, creamy milk, sweet hay, and sour corn mash all mixed together. She closed her eyes.

Jesus, Mary, and Joseph, keep Mama safe. Jesus, Mary, and Joseph, it's my fault, not hers.

Someone touched her back. Sophie turned her head and the rough hay scratched against her cheek. She opened her eyes.

Aunt Rae was sitting next to her.

Sophie sat straight up, blurted out, "What's wrong?"

"It's okay, Sophie. The bleeding has stopped."

"Mama's all right?"

"Anna is doing better, much better. Your mother is stubborn and strong. Holding her baby has made her even stronger."

Mama is doing better. Mama is holding on. Sophie closed her eyes a moment—*Thank you, dear God*—and then looked at her aunt. "How did you know I was up here?"

Aunt Rae picked up some loose hay and rolled it between her fingers. "I used to come up here when I was your age and was upset. I thought you might do the same."

"Here?" Sophie looked at her aunt. "I didn't know you liked the barn. Did Mama come here too?"

Aunt Rae shook her head. "No, not really."

A gray mouse with tiny black eyes scampered out from under a hay bale. It sniffed the hay, its nose twitching, its pink ears round like tiny translucent petals. Suddenly aware of its audience, the mouse froze for a moment, then scurried out of sight.

"I'm sorry, Sophie."

"For not letting me help?"

"For that"—Aunt Rae fidgeted, smoothed out her apron—"and for a lot of things." She looked at Sophie. "Nonna will need your help these next few months. Your mama's lucky to have someone like Nonna. And a daughter like you."

"Did Mama sing to Tony?"

"I ... I don't know, I really don't know. Why do you ask?"

"Nonna said mothers sing to their babies when they're born."

Aunt Rae looked down. "Your father and I took turns checking on you—you slept the whole afternoon and past supper. You must be hungry." She reached over to Sophie, touched her hand. Sophie pulled away.

"Where's Papa now?"

"Taking the doctor back to town."

"And the priest?"

Aunt Rae smiled. "Your father refused to get the priest. Said getting a priest was absolutely not necessary."

The loft suddenly felt small, as if the whole world had shrunk and only the two of them remained.

"What's happening at the house now?"

"When I left to come here, your mother was nursing Tony. She asked to see you. Nonna agreed, but not until after Anna rested."

Sophie took a deep breath, closed her eyes.

Mama was asking for me. I will see Mama soon.

"Nonna stays right near your mother, usually humming one of her opera songs. Your father hauled up her big old rocker from the kitchen so Nonna could sit and rest some." Aunt Rae paused, cleared her throat. "Sophie?" She hesitated, then said, "There was something you mentioned about Karl's father ..."

"Yes?"

"He was hurt in the war? Do you know if he was fighting in Italy?"

Sophie shook her head, confused. "I don't know."

Aunt Rae took a quick breath; then words began to spill out. "I really am sorry for what I said, Sophie, about Karl. I was scared. And the war. It seems we never know how much we care about someone until ... sometimes it's too late." She hesitated. "Long ago I was scared like this."

Sophie stared at her aunt. "Like this? What do you mean?"

"Scared of losing what we love." Aunt Rae shook her head. "I guess you are getting old enough now. Old enough to understand about ..." She looked away.

"About what?"

"About family. About things we don't talk about."

"What kind of things?"

"There was someone once." Aunt Rae turned to Sophie. "I wish you could have met him. But I lost him."

"In the war?"

Aunt Rae nodded, fiddled with the hay in her hand. "Alessandro. His name was Alessandro."

"Alessandro?" Sophie repeated. The soft syllables rolled off her tongue.

Today Sophie had been terrified that she might lose what she loved most—her mama, her family.

"I'm sorry," Sophie said.

Aunt Rae gave a little start. Already a frown was back on her face. "Never mind, Sophie. I was just upset, this long day, and so tired. Karl and his father. Alessandro leaving for war. So many memories jumbled together."

Aunt Rae poked back dark strands of hair that curled around her face. "And now this new baby." She tried to smile. "Not a word of this to your mother, Sophie. It might upset her. Promise, not one word."

Pale China Plate

Sophie had paused at the top of the stairs, her eyes fixed on her mother's bedroom door, when suddenly Nonna backed out of the room, cradling Tony in one bent arm. She closed the door behind her and then turned around.

"Oh! You surprised me," Nonna said to Sophie. "See? Our *bambino*! You sang to him. He stays."

"Nonna, can I ask you something?"

"*Sì.*"

"Did you know Alessandro?"

Nonna raised her eyebrows. "Alessandro?"

"Aunt Rae told me about him."

Nonna hesitated. "We will talk later. Your mama, she is waiting. Go! Go!"

Sophie carefully opened the bedroom door, stepped in, and looked at her mother. Her heart began racing.

Her mother's face was white, pale and fragile like a china plate. Blue veins crisscrossed her forehead. Her hair was damp and matted.

Sophie clenched her fists. It was all she could do not to

burst into tears. Her mother stirred.

"Mama?"

Her mother's eyes fluttered open for a moment and then closed, as if staying open was just too hard.

"Sophie, come here." Mama's hands lay across her chest, not moving, her fingers still and limp. Mama's hands were always busy, snapping peas, stitching a ripped hem, doing one chore or another.

"I'm sorry, Mama, so sorry ..."

"Hush, Sophie ... not your fault ... no one's." Between breaths, she rested. "Sophie ... come close ... here ... near me."

Mama looked at Sophie with eyes so blue, so clear, but distant, like faraway sky.

Sophie touched her mother's hand. Her mother smiled faintly. Sophie's heart hurt, actually hurt. "Mama, you are going to be all right. You are."

Her mother's eyes widened. Mama was watching Sophie the way she did some evenings after the last of the supper dishes had been dried and put away. She would stand as still as stone and gaze as if Sophie was about to disappear.

Mama's fingers inched across the bedsheet until they touched Sophie's hand. "I love you, Sophie." Mama rested a moment. "Don't ... don't be afraid. So good ... you are here."

Sophie kissed the tips of her mother's fingers. Her own hands were shaking. Sweat trickled down Mama's face and beaded across her forehead.

Mama, hold on. Mama. I need you.

There was a basin of water on the bed stand and a cloth. Sophie rinsed the cloth in the cool water, wiped the sweat off her mother's forehead.

"Thank you," her mother whispered. Her breathing was shallow and rapid as if she couldn't get enough air. "I need to rest."

"I love you, Mama," Sophie whispered.

Mama tried to open her eyes but couldn't. "I love you too."

Sophie turned and hurried out of the room. All she could see was her mother's colorless face.

Hold on. Please hold on.

Voices drifted up from the kitchen. Sophie paused at the top of the stairs, straining to hear, but she couldn't pick out the words, or even the voices for sure. She could hear her father muttering, and she thought she could make out Aunt Rae's cranky voice. Whatever they were saying must be important, judging by the way their words flew at each other. She moved down the stairs quietly, not wanting to be heard.

"Someone needs to tell her. Now."

That was Papa's voice. Sophie was close enough now to hear the words.

"*Sì*, we must. But now? No."

"Then when? She has a right to know."

"*Sì*, I understand."

"She is stronger than we think. She's ready."

Papa sounded so angry. What were they arguing about?

"First Anna must be stronger."

"Promise you'll talk to her soon, Rae."

Sophie couldn't keep quiet any longer. She stepped into the kitchen. Papa, Nonna, and Aunt Rae were all clustered near the sink, their backs to Sophie.

"Talk to who? Me?" she asked.

Everyone turned. Papa and Aunt Rae stared as if Sophie had suddenly grown horns.

Nonna glared at Aunt Rae, then uttered a volley of Italian so fast Sophie could not understand one word.

"What were you talking about?"

"Nothing, Sophie," Aunt Rae said.

"But I heard you—"

"Nothing that needs discussing right now."

"Is there something wrong with Mama? With the baby?"

"No." Papa glanced at Aunt Rae, who looked away.

"What is it? Why won't you just tell me?"

"Sophie, you are right, some things need telling. But now is not the right time."

"When is the right time?"

"I'm sorry, Sophie," Papa answered gently. "It's not for me to say."

A Different Stone

All the next day Sophie kept busy helping Aunt Rae and Nonna. While they took care of her mother and the baby, her job was keeping the household going—fixing meals, mixing the bread dough, boiling water for washing sheets and diapers. There seemed to be no end to what needed to be done, and it was nearly suppertime before Sophie could slip outside. Papa and Karl would be finishing up the afternoon's plowing soon.

Sophie breathed in a long, deep breath and then another. The air in the orchard was wonderfully fresh, cool against her face; it even smelled green. Being away from the house made the world feel bigger, brighter, and not so closed in.

She spied Karl's tall, thin silhouette near the field. She walked a bit faster.

Karl smiled when he saw her. "I can only stay a few minutes. Ma's waiting dinner for me. I was hoping I might see you and make sure you're doing okay."

Sophie pressed her hands against her apron.

"Is something wrong? You look worried."

"So much has happened. I can't figure it out."

"Your mother, is she all right?"

"I don't know." Sophie looked away.

"That must be hard, really hard."

"Everyone is acting so strange ... and ..."

"And what, Sophie?"

"Mama looks so weak." Sophie clenched her hands, trying to stop the trembling. She looked up at Karl.

"What is it, Sophie?"

"No one will answer my questions or tell me anything. Even Aunt Rae is saying things that don't make any sense."

Karl nodded. "Sometimes what people say when they're scared doesn't make sense. I was little when Papa came back from the war. He'd been in the hospital a long time because of losing his arm. I'll never forget how strange Ma got, waiting for him, knowing he'd been hurt. One minute she'd be so strong, the next minute she'd be crying. That scared me more than anything."

Sophie closed her eyes a moment and listened to Karl's words.

"Sometimes it's hard to understand people's way of being upset. With everything that's happening, I ... I want you to know, I'm here for you, Sophia Rose."

Startled by the gentleness in his voice, Sophie's eyes opened, grew wide.

"And if I can't be here in person, hold on to this." Karl placed a small packet in her hand.

"Go ahead. Open it. It's for you."

As she unfolded the cream-colored paper, a small stone

slipped out. It was a deep pink, polished smooth and shaped like a heart. She rubbed the stone with her fingertips and looked back up at Karl. "Thank you. It's lovely."

She looked more carefully at the paper and turned it over. On one side there were several lines of writing, carefully inked in black. But the words were foreign. She looked up again, puzzled.

"The words are from a song my mother used to sing," Karl said.

"What do the words mean?"

He looked embarrassed. "The words are Czech, my parents' language. Someday I'll tell you."

"Thank you, Karl. Thank you." Sophie felt flustered and didn't know what else to say. She refolded the paper exactly as it had been and tucked the stone and paper in her apron pocket.

"The stone is marble, from the Alps. My father brought a box of them back from Italy, after the war. He showed me how to polish them."

"It's ... it's very special." She glanced at Karl, then looked away. "I will keep it here in this pocket, close to me."

Karl smiled, a big smile.

She felt happy, all bubbly inside, but more than that, sort of silly and giddy.

Then she heard someone calling her name, someone from the house.

"That's Rae, my aunt." Sophie couldn't help shaking her

head. "Not the easiest person to get along with, but she did apologize about how she behaved yesterday when you brought over the soup and bread."

Aunt Rae called again, louder, and then a different voice boomed out. Her father's voice.

"I'm coming, I'm coming!" Sophie called back, and then said to Karl, "I'd better go."

He gave a little bow. "See you tomorrow?"

Sophie touched the stone in her pocket. "Yes. Tomorrow."

A Story to Tell

Papa stood alone on the front porch. Aunt Rae must have gone inside.

"Sophie, come sit with me. Soon I'll need to go back to the barn and check on a couple of the cows. It was hard on them to go so long between milkings. But first, let's talk."

Papa was smiling. His face looked like her papa's face again, not full of tired wrinkles. His eyes had their usual twinkle as if he was thinking about doing something he shouldn't. Mama must doing better, she must be.

Sophie sat down next to her father on the porch swing.

"Sophie, we've all had a rough time of it these past couple of days."

Back and forth they rocked as she waited for him to continue.

"Yes, your mama's going to be all right. It'll take some time, but healing's on its way. For that we can all be mighty thankful." Papa pushed back his worn black hat. "I may be just a farmer, but I do know a few things besides plowing and milking cows." He gave a little nod. "Like knowing when a fresh pie is a good one just by the smell of it. Come to think of it, I haven't seen any signs of a pie around here for a long spell."

Sophie gave her papa a punch on the arm. Her whole world felt a lot lighter with Papa teasing again.

"Thanks for coming back up to the porch soon as we called." He nodded toward the kitchen. "Especially before Rae headed down there, which she was about to do." Papa cleared his throat. "I think she's a little suspicious there's something more interesting than apples down in the orchard."

"Papa!"

"Something also tells me she didn't take a liking to your young man."

"He's not 'my young man.'" She thought about what was in her pocket.

"Go a little easy on Rae, Sophie."

"What do you mean?"

Papa rubbed the rough stubble on his chin. "Some things need explaining, but I'm not the one for the job. I'm sorry, Sophie, I truly am. I'm asking you to be patient with us. We need to get through these next few days and let things simmer down. Okay?"

"Okay."

Papa rearranged his hat on his head, peered down toward the cow corral. "My barn ladies are still upset about their routine being disturbed. Can't say I blame them. I could use some help getting them settled for the night."

Ambling down to the barn next to her papa felt familiar

and good. The cows were standing around the outside feed racks, mooing their complaints, every face looking right at them. "I guess they deserve a few extra flicks of hay," Papa said. But before he slid back the heavy barn door, he paused. "About that discussion in the kitchen ..."

Sophie was startled when Papa's voice changed from teasing to serious, even a little sad. "Sometimes we have to accept that life doesn't always go the way we want it to." He looked at his daughter. "The hard part is being at peace with what we can't change."

It was strange for her father to do so much talking. Especially when she couldn't understand what he was getting at.

"I'm sorry, Papa, about the pigs and not feeding them."

"No, Sophie. That's not what I was talking about."

The cows were tired of waiting. Their mournful lamentations had steadily grown louder. Papa didn't seem to notice. He stood with his hands in his pockets, his jaw working, a sure sign he was figuring out how to say something more.

"I've come to learn this, Sophie—the sun shows its face every morning, regardless of what happened during the night. Sometimes I wish I could slow it down or hurry it up, but there's no use wishing either way. The sun takes its own sweet time. Maybe it's got more sense than any of us. Instead of tasting what's filling our mouths today, we worry about tomorrow, worry over things we can't change, like spilt milk. No matter how much we wish it, no amount of regrets will put that milk back in the pail." Papa shrugged and looked at Sophie with an embarrassed grin. "Sometimes I talk too much once I get started." He pushed hard on the barn door and slid it open.

Sophie walked over to Bossie, knuckled the heifer's head in that flat space between her wide-set eyes. "I don't know what Papa was talking about, Bossie. But listen to this, Mama's better. Papa said so."

Sophie kept thinking about her papa's words. The cow kept chewing her cud, same slow, steady rhythm, jaws slurping side to side.

Sophie reached into her pocket. Her fingers touched the smooth stone. It was there, safe and solid. Tomorrow would be coming soon.

Sing!

The next day crawled by. Each time she finished one set of chores, her aunt assigned another. Sophie wanted to slip past Rae's watchful eyes and hightail it down to the orchard. Karl was helping Papa plow. It would be fun to wave hello if nothing else. But when the potatoes were peeled and the garlic chopped, Aunt Rae handed her a laundry basket of diapers. After that, Mama's sheets had to be changed, wood had to be carried in and stacked ... and then it was already suppertime.

Finally, dinner was eaten, evening dishes were done. Aunt Rae took Tony up to Mama for nursing. Nonna was folding diapers. Papa was already down at the barn starting the evening milking. Sophie grabbed her shawl off the hook and scooted out the door.

She wandered between the old apple trees. The orchard smelled fresh and full of spring. The air had lost its cold bite, and the pear and apricot trees had changed into shimmering umbrellas of pale blossoms—already, so quickly! Sophie paused as she wandered past the row of headstones. Two large white ones and three small gray ones. She was surprised at the rush of sadness that choked up her throat. She blessed herself with a quick sign of the cross and hurried further down the orchard.

There was Karl standing by the fence. Sophie couldn't help but smile. "Thanks for coming by, especially after a full day of school and then helping Papa. Tonight I can't stay very long, Karl. Aunt Rae wants me to help her with something—can't remember what, but first she went upstairs to visit with Mama and the baby."

"How's your ma?"

"Doing better."

"And the baby?"

"Making lots of laundry."

Karl laughed. "I'm not getting you into trouble by showing up here?"

"Why should having a little conversation cause trouble?" Sophie didn't mean to sound angry, but even though she had every right to be in the orchard talking to Karl, she felt guilty about it.

"I've brought a list of assignments in case you have time to think about homework. Miss Tryner sends her regards."

"Thanks."

"People at school are asking about you and your family. Wondering how you're doing."

"Oh, Karl, I can't believe anyone has even noticed. Anyway, I should be back next week if the baby keeps doing well and Mama gets a little more strength."

"You are missed."

Sophie broke off a twig from an overhead branch. She twirled it back and forth.

Karl looked toward the house. "I think I hear someone calling."

"Already!" Sophie glanced up the hill. Yes, that was Aunt Rae's voice. "Karl, I'm sorry, I'd better hurry back home."

The porch light flickered on. Rae's voice rang out. "Sophie! It's getting dark."

Karl gave a little bow. "Good night, Sophia Rose. See you tomorrow?"

"Yes, that would be nice." Sophie hesitated. "Yes, very nice." She turned, ducked under some branches, and hurried home.

Rae was standing straight as a statue as Sophie rushed up to the house. Nonna was sitting on the porch swing, rocking the baby, humming a lullaby.

"You were gone a long time, young lady. Not a safe time to be walking down there"—Aunt Rae cleared her throat—"especially alone. A lot could happen."

"Nothing happened."

The baby began to fuss.

"Take little Tony to your mother," Nonna said to Sophie. "He's ready to eat and—"

"I'll take the baby up," Aunt Rae interrupted.

"No. I asked Sophie to take him to Anna. She's been asking to see her daughter."

Aunt Rae didn't argue. Her mouth stayed shut.

Nonna placed the baby in Sophie's arms and waved her on. "Stay and visit with your mother." Nonna frowned at Aunt Rae. "*We* will talk."

Sophie held her brother carefully, cradled in her arms, all bundled up in a warm blanket. The baby was squirming, fussing a little, but not crying. Sophie hurried up the stairs as fast as she dared. She knocked softly, then pushed open the bedroom door.

"Mama?" She peeked in. "Are you awake, Mama? It's me, Sophie. The baby needs you."

"Come here, Sophie. I've missed you."

Mama's face was still pale, but her eyes were bright. She was sitting up in bed, pillows stacked behind her. She patted a place right next to her. Sophie handed her the baby and sat down.

"Thank you, Sophie. How do you like holding your brother?"

"He's a little squirmy but beautiful."

"*You're* beautiful. Papa's been telling me what a fine help you've been." Her mother reached over and tucked back some loose curls.

The baby whimpered. Mama looked down and smiled at the baby's pink frowning lips. "Excuse me, Sophie, I'll let him start nursing, and then we can visit, just the two of us. Seems like it's been a long time."

Mama lifted aside a lace shawl and then eased Antonio's eager mouth to her breast. Sophie looked away. She had seen plenty of barn animals nursing their young, but this was entirely different.

Antonio made soft sounds, sucking and swallowing. His entire little body seemed concentrated on eating. His tiny hand reached along Mama's breast. She touched his palm, and his fingers curled right around hers. Sophie remembered what Nonna had said the night he was born. *This baby must know he is loved something powerful*, Sophie thought.

"Tony's dark curls remind me of yours, Sophie, when you were born."

"Is that how I looked?"

"Oh, you were never quite this little. You arrived hollering and strong, ready to take on the world." Mama took in a few long, slow breaths and then whispered, "I especially remember your eyes, so big and dark. You were always looking around wanting to find things out."

"Did you sing to me?"

Mama blinked, looking startled, and said, "Did I sing to you?"

"Nonna said when you sing to a baby you call to its soul. When I sang to Antonio, he looked right at me, almost clear *into* me."

Mama's smile faded to a soft sadness. "Nonna sang to all my babies." And then she looked away.

"I'm sorry, Mama, I didn't mean to upset you."

"No, it's good to be talking. We have so much more to talk about, so much I want to tell you. A new baby stirs up the memories of past ones." Antonio squirmed but didn't stop nursing. Mama wiped away a bit of milk dripping down his chin. "It's hard talking about ... my babies. I never stop thinking about them, not for one day." Mama swallowed hard.

"And I never stop thinking about you, Sophie." Mama paused. "Papa and I have waited a long time for this baby. He needed everyone singing him to stay. Thank you." Mama let go of Tony's curled-up fingers and squeezed Sophie's hand.

Antonio gave a little cry, and Mama placed him upright, his head on her shoulder, and patted his back.

Then Mama pulled Sophie close to her. "My dear, dear Sophie."

Sophie closed her eyes and breathed in the good smells of baby, sweet soap, and lavender oil. They both were quiet. That tight knot in Sophie's heart finally began to loosen.

Sophie stirred, straightened back up. "Mama?"

"Yes?"

"Papa, Nonna, and Aunt Rae were arguing about something that seemed important."

"What was that?" Mama shifted so she could look directly at Sophie.

"I don't know. Something I needed to be told, they said. Papa said it wasn't his to talk about. Is there something wrong? With Tony? With me?"

Her mother answered slowly, "Sophie, we're all so worn

out from worrying. There is nothing wrong. Nothing! We love you, Sophie. You know that, don't you? Nothing will ever change that."

"Of course." She was about to say more, but her mother was out of breath and her face was again pale and drained. Tears had collected in the corner of her eyes.

"I'm tired, so tired, Sophie. The baby's sleeping. Would you take him down to Nonna?"

Sophie tiptoed out of the room, holding her little brother close to her chest. That felt good and reassuring, but all around the edges she felt worried—and something else: sad. As if she had lost something, but had no idea what it was.

Ragtime

The next day was another long day of chores. Time seemed to be playing tricks on her. So much had happened, and yet it had been only a few days since Tony's birth. Every day felt endless. More laundry, more dirty diapers, buckets of water to boil and carry outside to the scrub board, hands turning raw and red from the strong lye soap. Finally Sophie's favorite part, hanging everything in long, straight rows on the laundry line. It felt good to be outside—to hear the clothes flapping in the wind, smell the fresh air, and feel the sunshine on her face. From time to time Sophie reached into her apron pocket, felt the stone's smooth sides, and smiled.

Whenever she had a few free minutes Sophie peeked into her mother's bedroom, hoping to talk some more. But either her mother was sleeping or Nonna or Rae were bustling around the room. Sometimes Nonna had the Victrola cranked full volume, playing one of Mama's favorite songs.

After the family's big middle-of-the-day meal, Sophie cleaned the kitchen, gazing out the window from time to time. Dark clouds had piled thick along the horizon. A breeze was kicking up, cold and gusty. She hurried out to gather in the laundry, but by the time she headed back to the house with a basket heaped high with damp diapers, the clouds had blown past and the sky was clear. When she got to the porch, she was surprised to see Aunt Rae buttoning her coat.

"Sophie, I need to walk over to the Kowalskis' for a couple of pints of goat's milk. Nonna thinks it will be good for Anna."

"I can get it."

"No. You stay here and keep an eye on the baby. He just finished nursing, so he should sleep now for at least an hour or two. Anna and Nonna are both napping. Your father is out plowing and won't be back until dark. Besides, I want to thank Mrs. Kowalski for the soup and bread." Aunt Rae tied a red silk scarf around her head. "And if Mr. Kowalski is home, I might say hello, tell him what a fine help his son has been with the spring plowing, and … and maybe ask him a few questions."

Sophie wasn't sure she had heard right, since her aunt had half swallowed the last few words. "Questions? About what?"

"Nothing special. About the war. Be sure to stir the tomato sauce from time to time so it doesn't scorch." Aunt Rae didn't nod good-bye or pause for even a moment. She marched off, head up, back straight, to the end of the drive and then turned onto the road.

Sophie watched her aunt depart. How different Mama and Rae were. Mama said that when they were growing up, Rae had been the wild one, always ready to try something new. Even went off to Chicago to get a teaching certificate.

People sure change.

Sophie picked up the laundry basket, pushed open the kitchen door, careful to keep it from slamming, and set the basket by the stove. She peeked in the warming oven and then propped the door open the way Nonna had showed her. Tony was sleeping, breathing slow and steady. The kitchen was quiet except for the clock's ticking, which didn't sound harsh and scolding today.

Sophie turned the radio on softly, sat at the kitchen table, closed her eyes, and listened. She should be peeling carrots for tonight's soup or rolling out the pasta dough. Instead she opened her math book and stared at the long list of assignments.

"Is the baby okay?"

Sophie jumped. Aunt Rae stood in the doorway holding a large basket filled with spring greens, several pint jars of goat's milk, a quart of beets, and a pie tin.

Sophie sat bolt upright. "Yes, the baby's fine."

Aunt Rae set the basket on the table, then walked over to the sink and began pumping water to wash the greens.

"Is Anna still sleeping? Did Nonna get some rest? And the sauce, did you keep it stirred?" Aunt Rae's words rolled out in a rapid staccato.

"Everyone's doing fine. Slept the whole time."

Aunt Rae turned, wiped her wet hands on her apron, and looked at Sophie. "Thank you." Her voice softened. "It was good to get out for a bit. Mrs. Kowalski insisted on sending back a rhubarb pie still warm from the oven and a quart of pickled beets. What have you been up to?"

"Working out some math."

"You enjoy that kind of thinking, don't you? Like someone else I knew. "

"Who was that?"

Aunt Rae just shook her head. "Is that the radio I hear?"

"I turned it on really low so it wouldn't disturb anyone. Listen—'Alexander's Ragtime Band' just started, one of Mama's favorites. Shall I turn it up a little louder?"

Sophie started humming with the lively music. *Come on along ... Come on and hear, Alexander's Ragtime Band.*

Aunt Rae gave a little gasp. Her hands flew up to her mouth.

"What's the matter, Aunt Rae?"

"I'm sorry. I don't know what's gotten into me. Being at the Kowalskis', now hearing that song. It reminded me of someone."

Sophie hesitated, then asked, "You mean Alessandro?"

Aunt Rae became quiet. They both listened until the song played out.

"That song. Reminds me of evenings when your mother was just out of high school. We sat by the radio, hoping to hear news of the war ... listening to the newest songs and singing along. 'Alexander's Ragtime Band' was a favorite of Anna's."

"Were you both living here on the farm?"

Aunt Rae looked away, sort of stared at the window.

"Anna ... my little sister, with a face so pretty it made every young man's head turn, and a figure to match. Oh, little Anna, romantic and with her thoughts in the clouds half the time, but stubborn. Lord, could she be stubborn! After high school she moved to Chicago to live with me, but not for long. Meeting your father changed all that. They fell in love so fast it scared us all." Aunt Rae's foot continued tapping along with the music.

"Oh, tell me about them, how they met, please! Mama's never told any of the stories, and Papa says he can't remember."

"Maybe for a minute. I guess it won't do any harm. But that dough can't wait forever to be rolled out." Rae glanced at the clock. "I suppose there's enough time until supper."

"How did they meet?"

"That's a good story." Aunt Rae smiled. "They met at one of those old-fashioned box suppers, a fundraiser for the war effort. Your father bid for Anna's basket and got himself some mighty fine fried chicken—and even better, a spring bride. We teased Anna about what she put in that basket, some kind of love potion, maybe ..." Aunt Rae shook her head, hummed a bit of the song. "Alessandro sang that at their wedding. Played it on his fiddle and sang along."

"He was there?"

"Yes, he was there. Alessandro was my beau, and a very handsome one."

Sophie didn't say another word, even though she had a head full of questions. If her aunt got stopped, she might not start again.

"Oh my, I completely forgot—the baby …" Aunt Rae stood up.

"He's still sleeping. I can see him from here. Please, Aunt Rae, tell me more. What was Alessandro like?"

Aunt Rae sat down again. "All the young men around here, even your grandfather and his only brother, they all were eager to join up. Eager to be part of the war effort. Who knows why? They argued it was their duty to help their brothers in the homeland." She paused. "There was some truth to that."

"What about Papa?"

"Nonna made it clear to your papa that if he wanted to marry Anna, he had better stay put. Someone had to help keep the farm running."

"And Alessandro?"

Aunt Rae looked down. She clasped her hands in her lap but couldn't keep them still. "Alessandro was a dreamer, his head full of ideas and ambitions." Her eyes were moist, but a smile flickered across her face. "He was hoping to go someday to Illinois Normal College to become a teacher … and teach math, and coach." Aunt Rae smiled a real smile. "He sure loved baseball."

"What did he look like?" Sophie asked.

"Tall." Rae gave a little laugh. "Tall for an Italian anyway, tall and dark. His eyes were such a deep brown, and his lashes long and thick." Aunt Rae clapped her hands. "Oh, Sophie, why am I going on like this? Rattling these old bones in the closet? I know better. It's time to be fixing supper."

"Did he propose?"

Aunt Rae became still. "He left for the war." She swallowed, looked away. "He left right after your parents' wedding. He left before ..." Aunt Rae stopped, shook her head. "War means hard times, Sophie. For everyone, our family included. Bills were piling up, and there was no cash coming in. I was teaching in Chicago, good pay for a woman. I needed to hold on to that job. Once a woman married, she wasn't allowed to teach." Aunt Rae twisted the edge of her apron. "Yes, Alessandro proposed."

"Did you accept?"

"I told him I would marry him when he came back. The very day, if we could." Aunt Rae pressed her hands across her apron. "He never came back," she said, looking around the room as if searching for something. She saw the clock and stared at it. "October 23, 1918. Shot down at Marano, Italy, near Trieste. He was fighting with the Tenth Gruppo. Fighting. My Alessandro shooting a gun. Alessandro, he wept just seeing an animal in pain."

Tears trickled down Sophie's cheeks. She was afraid even to breathe and risk interrupting her aunt.

"The war ended only a few months later. What sense was there to any of it!" Aunt Rae paused, swallowed, then spoke barely above a whisper. "He's buried in Italy, alongside his comrades." She put one hand to her throat. "They say the cemetery's beautiful. White crosses. Rows and rows of white crosses. Soldiers who never came home."

Aunt Rae looked at Sophie, looked at her straight on. "Someday I will go there. Say how sorry I am for ... for everything, and say good-bye properly." She paused, cleared her throat. "He was a good man, Sophie. I wish you could have known him."

"I'm sorry, I mean—"

"I loved him." Aunt Rae smoothed out her apron. "I want you to know that."

Then Aunt Rae slapped her hands on her skirt, stood up. "Supper's not going to cook itself." She walked to the sink, dumped the dough on the cutting board, picked up the rolling pin, formed the dough into a ball, and rolled it out thinner and thinner. "Sophie," she asked without looking up, "go down to the cellar. I need another quart of tomatoes. And see if you can find some canned pears for tomorrow's dessert."

Down in the cellar Sophie stood surrounded by rows and rows of Nonna's canning—beets, peaches, green beans, corn. Green-tomato relish and dozens of quart jars of tomato sauce. The air was cool, spicy with smells of vinegar, dill, and garlic from the pickle crocks.

Garlic and dill. Rows of shiny jars. Alessandro singing ragtime at Mama and Papa's wedding. War. Rows and rows of white crosses, gray silent stones in the orchard.

A strange weariness filled Sophie. She sat down on Papa's three-legged stool, tucked her knees under her chin, circled her arms around her legs. And then, not knowing why, she cried and cried.

Smashed and Broken

There was no more mention of old times or the war. Alessandro's name was not spoken out loud. Aunt Rae's face stayed shut, as if a book had been closed. Papa tried teasing about the "Polish" rhubarb pie needing a little Italian sweetening, but even that didn't raise a hint of a smile. Supper that night was long and still.

The next day Aunt Rae seemed annoyed with everyone, especially Sophie, even though she tried to do everything her aunt asked.

"Sophie, come here and help. This laundry is not going to hang itself up. Goodness knows how one baby can make so much work."

"Here, let me carry that outside." Sophie reached for the heavy basket. For a moment her eyes locked with her aunt's. "I ... I wanted to ask ..."

"Ask what? If it has anything to do with yesterday's conversation, I don't want to talk about it." Aunt Rae yanked the basket away from Sophie. "What's done is done. I don't know what got into me yesterday. Just plain foolishness!"

Aunt Rae pushed open the kitchen door and let it slam. "You

carry out the rest of the wash. It's in the bucket by the sink." Then she strode across the porch, straight to the side yard. Sophie picked up the rest of the laundry and rushed to catch up. A dozen or so chickens were scratching in the soft dirt but scurried over to Sophie, who usually had a handful of crumbs.

Aunt Rae plunked down the basket. The chickens squawked, hopped a distance away with their feathers ruffled. She pulled out a handful of clothespins from her apron pocket and held several between her teeth while she snapped the rest onto the diapers that Sophie draped over the laundry line. Sophie didn't say a word.

During supper Sophie kept glancing at the clock, hoping no one would notice. Papa said Karl had offered to finish plowing the upper field. He should be done soon.

Sophie helped Nonna clean up the kitchen. "Dishes are done. Is there something else you'd like me to do?"

"Go, go. I can see you are in a hurry. You want to get to the orchard."

Sophie tried not to let her smile look too obvious.

Nonna nodded. "I know, I know." She clicked her tongue as a warning. "Don't be late. There is no sense to ruffle feathers in the henhouse. *Capisc*? You understand?"

"I'll be back before dark. I promise."

Sophie hurried down the path. It was too early for Karl to be there, but already her insides felt all jumpy, like when she was on that giant Ferris wheel in Chicago last summer. She and Papa got stuck nearly at the top, and then that giant wheel began turning. Up and over, except her stomach seemed to leap ahead. They could see everywhere, so far, the blue lake water spilling all the way to the horizon like how she imagined an ocean would look, full of big splashing waves and continuing on and on, almost to the end of the world. Her world, anyway.

Past the first row of trees, the air was cooler and all seemed hushed. The quiet of evening was settling over everything. Evening was her favorite time of the day. Or maybe morning was her favorite time. She liked them both. She felt free and safe here in the orchard, a place to find magic feathers when she was little, climb trees, hide in the branches, watch an inchworm move across a leaf. Or just sit and think with no one interrupting.

She searched out the big oak down at the far end of the orchard, the tree that marked her family's burying place. It was easy to spot the tall, twisty oak, which towered above the smaller fruit trees. She walked even faster. There they were. Beneath the tree she saw them—the gravestones. Her family.

She sat cross-legged in the soft spring grass near the first stone, the large white one. She searched through the clover for a lucky four-leaf. It would be fun to give one to Karl.

She looked more closely at the half-dozen stones. So many times she had sat here, thinking about them. When she was little, she'd make up stories. As she grew older, she wondered about these people she had never met. The oldest was Giuseppe, her grandfather. Nonna liked to tell how after they bought this farm, he had sent money back to an uncle to have his family's grand piano shipped all the way from Italy. It had cost a lot, but the piano was important to him. "Music is the language of the soul; we each find a way to sing. That is what he believed," Nonna had told her. "He left that for us, right here, *capisc*."

Sophie touched the smooth stone. Her grandfather's initials, *G.P.R.*, were carved across the stone, a silent square of white. "Beautiful marble from our homeland, the best, the finest," Nonna always said with pride, "for my Giuseppe."

He had died from the influenza somewhere out East, training for the Great War. Nonna said half the men in that Italian-American battalion died of the influenza. "Your grandfather, my Giuseppe, never fired a single shot. Never did he shoot another soldier, not one person." Then she would shake her head and say nothing more.

Next to his stone was another white stone. Three initials were carved on it: *A.P.R. 1892–1918*. Sophie traced the letters. *A.P.R.* Alessandro? She hadn't thought to ask Aunt Rae about his last name. But Aunt Rae said he was buried in Italy.

Then three gray stones. Three no-name babies. Sophie remembered the too-early baby boy they buried in September a few years back. She and Papa had walked down together. Mama couldn't come with them; she was still too weak. Nonna had stayed with her. About halfway there, Papa took hold of Sophie's hand, and she held on tight. They stood by the stone, not saying anything, staring at the little heap of earth piled nearby. They recited the Our Father. Papa made the sign of the cross, whispered, "I will always remember this little boy born in September...," and then picked up the shovel and covered the tiny wooden coffin with dirt. Sophie sat by the grave a long time with Papa. She didn't want to go back to the house where her mother sat, looking out the window, staring at somewhere far away.

The middle stone was for another baby boy. Sophie didn't remember him. She used to ask her mother about the no-name babies, but the answer was always, "Some other time, not now. Now is not a good time for talking."

A good time for talking never happened.

Papa said the baby girl was the first, the oldest. There were no dates on any of the gray stones.

Sophie stared at that oldest stone, wondering. Imagine having a sister, just like Mama and Rae had each other. Sophie had never imagined that girl baby as ever being real, a real sister—a little girl with a name. Funny how holding Tony had changed that. Tony's birth, and being able to hold a real baby, made everything different.

She'd be nearly grown, like me. Maybe she'd be petite and pretty like Mama, or tall like Papa, or maybe she'd play the piano like Aunt Rae.

Three stones. Three babies who hardly got started before they died.

Sophie traced the edge of each square, and then pressed her hands flat against the cold surface, one stone after another. "Hello, little brothers. Hello, big sister. Mama loves you. We all love you."

"Excuse me, I don't mean to interrupt."

Sophie looked up, startled. "Karl! How long have you been standing there? I didn't know you were here."

"Not long. Sorry if I gave you a start; I sure didn't mean to. I didn't want you to think I was eavesdropping."

Sophie stood up, brushed bits of grass and clover off her apron and smoothed back her dark wavy hair. Curls were always getting loose from the bun, no matter what she did. "I was, well, I know it sounds silly, I was just talking to myself."

"I like hearing your voice, even if you're just talking to yourself." Karl's face lit up as he smiled. "I brought something to show you."

He reached to his back pocket and pulled out a smooth piece of wood. "My pa made this for me."

Sophie looked closer. "A slingshot?" Her brow wrinkled up; she didn't quite know what to say. "Aren't you kind of old for a slingshot?"

"He made it for me before he left for the war. I was too little for it then. Ma put it away until he was back home."

Sophie took it from Karl and looked at it carefully, trying to be polite. It seemed like a strange thing to show her. "Do you use it?" She handed it back.

"Most every day. I don't shoot at anything alive. I have targets set up along the back fence." Karl turned a little red. "When I get good at shooting I'm going to show Pa." He stuck the slingshot back into his pocket. "I don't know. Maybe being a slingshot sharpshooter to please my father doesn't make much sense."

"A lot of things don't make sense anymore, Karl. Especially right now. I wish ..." She turned away.

"Hey, hold on there. What is it?"

"I don't understand about my Aunt Rae. I just can't figure her out. Mostly she's so glum and ornery, like a kid trying to pick a fight. She can say the meanest things, and I want to be mean right back. Gets me so riled up and mad. Then some-times, like when she's playing the piano, she becomes a dif-ferent person. Nonna says that's when her soul is singing. Or like yesterday, when she went on and on about Alessandro and the war. How can a person change back and forth like that?"

"That's how my pa is. Since the war."

"At least he came home."

"But he's never really come home. Not to us." Karl kicked at a clump of dirt. "Ma keeps trying."

"Maybe ... maybe it's too hard."

"The worst part is how he hates the way he is. Not being able to work the farm. Maybe it's the things he's seen and done. I don't know. He won't say anything. It's all shut up inside him." Karl scraped up a handful of rocks and starting throwing one after another. Then he stopped. "I've come to know this, Sophie. All those ugly memories inside my pa are like poison. They eat away at him, and then mean, hateful words pop out." Karl dropped the last rock, shook his head. "He hurts the people he says he cares about."

Sophie looked directly at Karl.

He reached toward her, took both her hands. She wanted to pull away. And then she closed her eyes, let the feelings swirl. Her head felt light and dizzy. The late-evening sun warmed the back of her head. Crickets were chirping; she hadn't noticed them before. The roosters down in the coop were crowing out their bravado.

Someone coughed, someone nearby. Sophie felt a sudden chill.

She opened her eyes. Karl had a puzzled expression on his face. They turned to look. Aunt Rae.

"I should have known. I turn my back and this is what happens."

Karl dropped Sophie's hands. He stepped back. "I'm sorry, ma'am. We were only ..."

"Only nothing! It's nearly dark, young man. You should be home."

"We were only talking," Sophie interrupted.

"You heard what I said. Leave. Now!"

"You have no right to speak to Karl like that," Sophie said to her aunt.

"It's all right, Sophie. It *is* time for me to be heading home." Karl took off his hat, gave a quick bow. "Please don't be angry with Sophie," he said to Aunt Rae. "We were only ..."

"Good night! Just leave."

"Good night, Sophie. I'm sorry."

Sophie watched Karl walk away, then turned to her aunt, furious, hands fisted, not knowing what to say first. "How dare you! Karl is my friend."

"You, young lady, march yourself up to the house."

"No!"

"Don't you get sassy with me. March right home. And if I ever catch you sneaking out again—"

"We weren't sneaking!"

"No more backtalk. Do what you're told."

"I will not."

Aunt Rae grabbed Sophie's wrist. "Go home, young lady. Now!"

Sophie pulled away. "You have no right to order me around like this. You're not my mother!"

Aunt Rae slapped Sophie across the face, hard. "Don't you *ever* say that to me. Just who *do* you think I am!" Suddenly her expression changed. Her hands flew up over her mouth. "Oh my dear God."

The slap burned Sophie's cheek. The words echoed in her head. *Just who* do *you think I am!* She couldn't take her eyes off her aunt's face.

"I'm sorry," Aunt Rae said. "So sorry for everything. Everything."

Sophie felt numb, hollow, as if she were watching from a distance. She heard the crickets. A bit of wind rustled the leaves. Cows bellowed. The milkhouse door slammed shut.

Aunt Rae's next words came out raspy, barely audible. "I never wanted it to be this way. Never."

Sophie turned and walked away.

Pale Ugly Skin

Sophie didn't care where she was walking, wasn't even aware. She didn't pay attention to the nervous clucking of the chickens or notice the distant barking that was growing louder . She might as well have been deaf.

Until the hush suddenly exploded. Yapping and howling. High-pitched cries. A bedlam of squealing pigs, screeching chickens.

Sophie stared into the darkness, confused. And then panic hit her. She understood. Wild dogs! A pack of wild dogs.

"Sophie!" her aunt's voice screamed from the darkness, from somewhere behind her.

"Dogs! It's those damn wild dogs again!" Papa yelled from up near the house.

"Sophie! Where's Sophie?" Even Nonna was shouting.

Sophie didn't know what to do, which way to run.

A chaos of growls, squeals, even the cows bellowing. Papa hollering. A rifle shot. Chickens screeched and squawked.

"You damn dogs get out of here!" Papa hollered. Another rifle shot.

Sophie pressed her hands over her ears. She couldn't get

her mind to think, to focus. It was too dark to see what was happening. Chickens were half running, half flying past her, squawking, feathers everywhere. Another gunshot. A dog yelping.

As suddenly as it had started, the pandemonium ended. The barking and yapping stopped as the dogs fled across the fields.

Papa hollered from near the chicken yard, "Sophie, if you're anywhere close, come down to the coop. I need help rounding up the chickens, what's left of them."

Hearing Papa call her name set Sophie in motion. She stumbled as she ran, tripping over tree roots and rocks.

The air in the coop was thick with swirling dust and bits of hay. Sophie put her apron over her mouth as she rushed toward the back wall, searching for any live chickens. Someone stumbled in, holding a kerosene lantern. Its oily smell permeated the space more than its dim light.

"Papa! The chickens, Mama's chickens. They're all—"

Sophie suddenly realized it wasn't Papa with the lantern. It was Aunt Rae. Her aunt moved silently through the dust-filled air almost like a ghost, the dim light of the lantern shimmering off swirls of hay and straw. She made halting progress toward the back of the coop and then stopped and set down the lantern.

Lifeless chickens, piled high, heaped one on top of another, had suffocated in their attempt to escape. Sophie knelt and lifted them up, one at a time, set them aside, reached for another. Rhode Island Reds, Mama's best layers. Then she heard a few soft cheeps from under the stack. Sophie pushed the rest of the chickens aside.

"Just look at that," Aunt Rae said, kneeling down near Sophie and scooping up one baby chick, then another. A half-dozen more were hiding under the lifeless pile. Somehow these little ones had survived, protected under their mothers. "Let's get these up to the house, let them settle down before they die from fright."

Aunt Rae grabbed a half-grown chick trying to make a quick escape, flapping its useless wings and running from the light.

"We'll put them in a crate under the stove, keep them warm and quiet," she added. "These chicks will do fine."

Sophie stared at her aunt.

Aunt Rae gathered her apron corners to make a nest. She picked up the lantern. "Soon as I hand them off to Nonna, I'll be back. There's nothing more to be done in here. Some of the hens went flying up in the trees. The dogs didn't get them all. The moon's coming up, take a look. See if your papa needs help catching them. I'll be back with the lantern as fast as I can."

Sure enough, at least a dozen chickens were roosting in the branches. The moon gave enough light so that Sophie could see their silhouettes. She went from tree to tree but couldn't get to any of them. She figured the chickens could stay where they were. They'd be safe until morning. At least she could tell Mama they hadn't lost the entire flock.

Then she heard a piercing squeal, almost a scream. The sow.

Papa shouted from somewhere by the barn, "Get back to the house! The dogs busted open the pen and the sow's loose, madder than hell. Looking for her sucklings."

Another scream, human this time. Her aunt. Sophie peered toward the barnyard. The faint gleam of the lantern showed near the corral.

Sophie ran, past the manure pile, the haystack, to the corral.

She grabbed a pitchfork that leaned against the fence. "Aunt Rae!" she yelled, running toward the bit of light from the lantern. "Aunt Rae!"

Her aunt stood next to the pig sty, her back to the barn. With one arm she held the lantern; with the other she clutched a squirming piglet. Across the sty was the sow. Moonlight shone on her pale pink skin. That sow was huge, ugly, and mad.

"Drop the pig," Sophie shouted. She held up the pitchfork, held it straight at the sow. Glancing toward her aunt, she repeated, "Drop it."

Aunt Rae's eyes were wide and scared. She didn't move. She seemed frozen.

The sow snorted, pawed the ground. Mud flew against the barn's side. That sow wanted her baby.

Don't look away. Hold tight. Get ready.

Sophie kept the fork's teeth aimed at the sow's head. Again she shouted, "Drop that pig. Now!"

The piglet squealed. But Aunt Rae still didn't move. Sophie tightened her grip on the pitchfork and walked slowly toward the sow.

"Rae, let it go!" Papa's voice boomed.

The sow squealed. A dull thump. The piglet ran past. Everything started spinning in strange slow motion. Sophie heard someone calling her name, someone nearby. She felt her father taking the pitchfork from her hands, then holding her close.

"It's okay, Sophie," he said gently. "The sow's run off, already hiding somewhere in the orchard. Her little ones are with her. We'll find them in the morning."

Papa stepped back and took Sophie by the arm.

"Let's go up to the house and let everything settle down a bit. Everyone's pretty upset, maybe especially your Aunt Rae."

Aunt Rae.

Willow Weep

Nonna wrapped Sophie in a warm blanket and sat her in the rocking chair, near the stove.

Papa smiled. "Pretty high-action evening, to be sure. The sow's still grunting her complaints somewhere out there in the dark."

It seemed to Sophie that everyone was staring at her. Papa stood by the door. Nonna sat across the table. Aunt Rae stood next to the chair. No one spoke. Soft peeps came from a box beneath the stove.

Sophie looked from person to person. She could tell. They knew what had happened. They knew about her, about Aunt Rae. They all knew.

For the next several days, Sophie and Aunt Rae avoided each other. If one was upstairs, the other stayed down; if Sophie went outside to feed the chickens, Aunt Rae stayed in the kitchen. Papa rushed from chore to chore, to check on Mama or fix another fence, drive into town to buy more corn seed, or haul milk to the creamery. Nonna didn't say anything to Sophie or Aunt Rae about their silence, their refusing to look at each other at the supper table, but Nonna was always watching. Her eyes noticed every little change. Sometimes Nonna would throw up her hands, sputter something in Italian, and walk off, shaking her head.

No one said anything about what had happened in the orchard.

Aunt Rae retreated to the parlor every evening. Her fingers did not fly over the keys now but picked across them slowly. Her music was somber, detached.

Sophie tried to stay away from the orchard, but she couldn't. She hoped Karl would appear, then was afraid that he would.

Often she was surprised to discover that she had drifted down to the graveyard and that she stood gazing at the unmarked stones.

Sometimes she sat in the shade of the tall oak, plucked blades of grass, and tossed them in the wind or rolled them between her fingers. Sometimes she reached into her apron pocket, unfolded the crinkly paper, studied the strange foreign words, and imagined what they might mean. She pressed the smooth pink stone between her palms, wondering what she would say if Karl were to duck under an apple bough, shake down a shower of petals, laugh and smile with his eyes, eyes as bright as a bluebird's feathers.

No one came to the orchard. No one laughed or called her name.

· · · ·

"Sophia, come help me. *Sì?*"

Nonna sat in the rocking chair on the porch, looking at the cornfields that were changing from furrows of shiny black to rows of fuzzy green.

"Music, we need music. Crank up the Victrola. *Per favore.*" Nonna smiled. "We will listen together."

"Which record?"

"Verdi. *Otello.*" Nonna smiled again, closed her eyes, and leaned back into the curve of the rocker.

"*Otello?* You've listened to it every day this week." Sophie frowned. "I don't understand what you like about it. Everyone dies."

Nonna shrugged. "*Sì.*"

On her way to the Victrola, Sophie walked past Aunt Rae. Their eyes met. They both stopped, stood still. Sophie looked at her aunt's pale face, the dark thick hair, stubborn, always a few loose curls. She touched her own hair. Aunt Rae looked away.

Sophie slowly walked back outside. "Nonna, were Alessandro and Aunt Rae ever married?"

Nonna stopped rocking. She looked at Sophie, raised her eyebrows. "No. They were betrothed. But never married."

Nonna paused, then continued, "*Vede*, important questions. You have heard some of the story. You need to hear it all, and you will, soon. Now, Sophia, we listen to the music."

She placed her hand on the porch swing near her. Sophie sat down.

"We must hear *italiano*, the beautiful language. *La lingua bellissima.*" Nonna tapped her chest. "Full of heart. Magnificent! The stories, they teach us. Today we will listen, we will learn."

Nonna looped a new skein of yarn around Sophie's hands and began unwinding. As she looped the yarn from the skein, she wound the wool into a ball, ready for knitting. Sophie sat. They both listened. The record played arias to the cornfields, to cows, pigs, and chickens, and to Sophie and Nonna.

When the overture finished, Nonna paused. She set down the yarn.

"*Sì*, I try to forgive," she said, ever so softly. "Like Desdemona." She tapped her head. "*Ma* no. I understand in my head, *capisc'*, but here"—she placed her hand on her chest—"I do not forgive. I try ... the heart, the head, they fight."

"Forgive who, Nonna?"

"My Giuseppe."

"Grandpa?"

"*Sì*, the music finds what I hide in my heart. We sing. We weep. We forgive. Each time a little more."

Sophie thought about "Ragtime Band," about her mother, Aunt Rae, and the night she sang to Tony.

"So, I tell you again about your grandfather, my Giuseppe." Nonna leaned back in the rocking chair. "He said to me, *I must go, I must fight. For my people, my father's people. This war, this Great War.*" She hummed and nodded, her lips saying the words as Desdemona sang. Nonna knew them all.

"War! What is it?" she continued. "Nothing, no sense. Sadness for women. Sadness to wear so heavy, day and night. I begged my Giuseppe, stay, stay. Our Anna, she is now with a first child. He says, *Italy must become free. I must help fight.*" Nonna looked at Sophie. "What good is this being free when our men, our children, are gone?"

Nonna shook her head. "My Giuseppe, he left. He did not fight. The terrible sickness took him."

Sophie could not take her eyes off her grandmother's face. She had never heard her talk quite this way.

"Your papa, Tony, he wants to go. But I tell him, you love our Anna? Then you stay! My Giuseppe, he is gone." Nonna took a deep breath; back and forth she slowly shook her head.

"Then Alessandro. He left." Nonna crossed herself, first her forehead, her heart, her shoulders. "Giuseppe ... Alessandro ... gone."

Nonna's voice had never sounded so heavy, so sad.

"We become ghosts left behind, walking first this room, then that room, pick up, set down." Nonna tapped her finger on the soft yarn.

"Finally, you are born. *Grazie a Dio.* We become alive. You bring hope. Our Sophia Rosa." Nonna closed her eyes, rocked back and forth as the music built to its finale.

"My Sophia, listen to this music. My Giuseppe says, language of our soul. This one says, forgive him, Nonna. Forgive your Giuseppe. Forgive. Sometimes it comes, sometimes it flies away." Nonna rocked a while, her hand on her heart, tapping, tapping to the rhythm of the song. "Desdemona, she forgives Otello everything." Nonna slowly nodded. "*Sì*. He kills her. Even this, even death, she forgives."

Nonna put her hand to her forehead, closed her eyes. Desdemona began her final song, *Willow, willow,* her mother's song, the song of death.

"I try. Every day. Like Desdemona. Forgive Giuseppe everything. Even that he died."

No-Name Baby

The next day Sophie waited until her mother and Aunt Rae had gone upstairs to rest after the big noon meal. Papa had gone into town. Tony was sleeping; already he looked bigger. Soon he would be two weeks old.

The house was quiet. She had been waiting for a chance to be alone like this with her grandmother.

She walked out to the porch, where she knew her grandmother was knitting. Nonna liked to do that on warm spring afternoons, pausing to look across the fields, sometimes talking to them.

"Nonna," Sophie asked, "is it true you write the names of everyone in our family in the Bible? Even the ones who died?"

Nonna nodded. "*Sì.*"

"My name too?"

"*Sì*," she answered slowly. "Your name is there too."

"May I see it?"

Nonna set down her knitting. She looked at her granddaughter, studied her face. "Are you certain you want to do this?"

"Yes," Sophie answered. "Aunt Rae said something a few days ago. Maybe I misunderstood, maybe not. I need to know."

"*Sì*, this is a good time, a quiet time." Nonna stood up, walked into the kitchen. She returned to the porch and handed Sophie a small silver key. "This will unlock the cabinet. Shall I come with you?"

"Thank you, Nonna, but I want to do this myself."

Nonna nodded. "Sometimes the things we must do are hard. But you are ready. I will wait here."

Even though she had Nonna's permission to be there, Sophie went into the parlor on tiptoes. The parlor was a mysterious place, a forbidden place. She hurried past the piano to the tall cabinet and unlocked its glass door.

Sophie took out the large, leather-bound book, their family Bible, and set it on the polished dining room table.

Nonna's handwriting was easy to recognize. The tall, slender letters were carefully written in black ink. Some words were in Italian.

She found Grandpa's and Nonna's names in the middle of the page: *Giuseppe Pietra Rossini—Elizabeth Maria Vacca.* Beneath their names a short line led to her mother's name, *Anna Sophia Rossini.*

A line connected Mama's name to Papa's: *Antonio Joseph Berta.* And then the date of their marriage: *June 12, 1918.*

Beneath their names were listed three births, three no-name babies:

Baby Girl Berta January 5, 1919
Baby Boy Berta March 10, 1922
Baby Boy Berta September 22, 1929

And then a new entry:

Antonio Giuseppe Berta April 8, 1932

My new little brother, Sophie thought. *My brother's name is here. But not my name. My name is not here.*

Sophie looked again at her mother's name. To the side was written another name—of course, Mama's sister: *Regina Maria Rose Rossini.* Aunt Rae's full name. And then no marriage line, just a man's name, with dates: *Alessandro Paul Romano (1892–1918).*

Underneath those two names was a single entry:

Sophia Rose Rossini February 10, 1919

Pecked to Death

Sunlight streamed through the open door of the hayloft. The air glowed. Swallows darted like dark arrows from their nests. Back and forth they flew through the high square window.

Sophie gazed out the door. Fields and pastures spread to the horizon. Muddy browns and blacks of early spring had become a dozen different shades of green. How completely the colors had changed since that long-ago morning when she peered through that circle of clear on her frosted window.

Down below, someone pushed open the sliding barn door. Footsteps clumped toward the ladder.

Papa's head poked through the square opening. He climbed up and then sat down on a hay bale.

"Nonna has supper ready. There's a heap of good food that you're missing."

"I'm not hungry."

"Your mama's been asking about you."

Sophie shrugged.

"Rae told me about ... about what happened in the orchard."

"Why didn't anyone tell me the truth?" Sophie looked at her father. "No one."

"I guess we were all too scared. We didn't know how to explain."

"I don't understand, Papa. I don't understand any of it."

Papa wiped his face with his shirtsleeve. "Seems that people behave no better than chickens. Pecking to death anyone that's different. Rae knew."

"Knew what?" Sophie ran a finger along a crack in the floor.

"Kids, teachers ... people. Mean, hurtin' words." Papa shook his head. "Rae had seen plenty of it—teasing and bullying on the playground. *Bastard child. Got no papa? Dumb immigrant wop.*"

"She could have married Alessandro."

Papa took a deep, long breath. "She needed to keep teaching, to keep the farm from going under. Those were hard times."

"Who knows about me?"

"Just us, our family. No one else."

"Why didn't anyone tell me?"

"Foolishness, Sophie. We were trying to protect you."

Sophie picked up a blade of straw, poked it at a knothole in the floor.

"When Rae realized the predicament she was in, she came here, to the farm. She took a leave from teaching. She told them she needed to help care for her sister. That was a reasonable thing to do—Anna was sick every day, so of course she needed her sister's help. Rae's other reason for coming here … was for no one to know. A farm in winter is its own island, isolated. Snow was deep that winter. No reason for Rae to go to town. Reasonable that I was the only one to saddle up the horse and push through the drifts."

"And then?" Sophie's words came out angry.

Papa waited. "Give me a minute here, Sophie. Be gentle with yourself. And with the rest of us. Neither you nor I have walked in Rae's shoes."

Sophie winced. A part of her still hoped she would wake up and everything would be as it was.

"That whole year nothing went right. Your grandpa's death and Alessandro's were hard enough. But then losing our child." Papa's eyes were swimming in tears. Papa's blue eyes. Mama's blue eyes. Sophie's brown eyes—like Aunt Rae's. Sophie had never noticed before.

"Our baby was born too early, too small. A beautiful baby girl. That winter night in early January, and all the next day, the temperature never broke zero."

Papa swallowed, his hands twisting a bit of twine. "Your mother took it so hard. Our little girl—gone. Alessandro and your grandpa, gone. The influenza took so many. Nonna had always been a rock to count on. She … for a while we were lost, all of us."

Papa breathed in, long and slow again, threw away the twine. "Then in February, you were born. The sun came out."

February. Sophie listened hard, not wanting to miss one word. She sat still and straight.

"Anna stayed with Rae the night you were born, never left her side. When we heard your first cry, loud and strong, we wept." Papa stopped, swallowed, stared at the loft window. "Your grandma was the first to shake off the sorrow. Then one by one, like coming out of some deep sleep, we started to come alive. Except Anna."

"Who decided about ... about me?"

"Anna couldn't let go—couldn't accept that our little girl was gone."

Papa sniffed and paused. Sophie waited until Papa could talk some more.

"The morning of your baptizing, Rae said to us point-blank, 'I've decided. If you two are willing, I am asking you to raise my child. As your own daughter. Your own, for always. No one, except family, needs to know. No one.'"

"But why? Why did she give me up?" Sophie swallowed, waited.

Her father coughed, cleared his throat, then continued. "Because of what she believed, because of what she said next. 'You two can give her a good life. I cannot.'"

Papa gently put his hands on Sophie's shoulders. "We took you as our own." He waited until Sophie looked up at him. "That's what you'll always be. Our own."

"You mean it, Papa? You really mean it?"

"Mean what, Sophie?"

"Now that I know, you're not going to send me away?"

"Sophie, Sophie, is that what you've been fretting about? There's no giving away something that's part of you. That would be worse than giving away my heart."

Sophie felt something tight and burning finally ease inside her. Tears welled up, and there was no stopping them.

Papa kept his arms around Sophie and let her cry and cry. Neither knew how long. Didn't matter. Papa held Sophie.

When she calmed, Papa looked at her and said, "This I do know. Rae loves you. As fierce as any mother loves her child. I've seen the terrible hurt and yearning on her face each time you run past her into Anna's arms. Rae's decisions were hers to know and understand. And live with. I've respected her, every single day, for her courage."

"Courage?"

"Yes, courage. There can't be anything harder than letting go of what you love."

Sing to Me

The next morning, when she was on her way back from feeding the chickens, Sophie heard piano music coming from the parlor. She walked across the porch and opened the kitchen door to make sure. How strange—Aunt Rae never played in the morning.

Sophie hurried into the kitchen, nearly tripping over two suitcases by the door. Startled, she looked around the room. Her mother was sitting in the rocking chair near the stove.

"Mama, what are you doing down here?" Sophie rushed over. "I'm sorry, I mean, are you really strong enough? Is it too cold? Should I get a blanket?"

"My Sophie is looking so grown up all of a sudden."

"Mama ... can I still call you that, or ...?"

"Oh, Sophie." Her mother stood up, wrapped her arms around Sophie, and held her close. "I am your mother. Always your mother. Our family has changed. Yes, big changes. You have a little brother. And we have"—Mama hugged Sophie an extra squeeze—"nothing more to hide."

The music from the parlor washed over them both.

Sophie gestured toward the suitcases. "Aunt Rae's?"

"I tried to talk her into staying. My sister is mighty stubborn. I guess we all are. I asked her to play the piano once more before she left."

Sophie looked at the door to the parlor, looked back at her mother. "I was going to tell Aunt Rae ... I don't know. That I'm all right."

Her mother nodded. "Go on."

Sophie slowly opened the parlor door. Part of her wanted to step inside. Part of her wanted to run away.

Her heart hurt something fierce. She stepped inside.

Aunt Rae glanced up. Her fingers stopped, suspended over the keyboard. "Yes, Sophie?"

"I saw your suitcases. In the kitchen."

"Don't worry, I won't interfere anymore. I am leaving on the afternoon train." Her fingers returned to their places on the piano, to the soft white keys. She played several notes and then stopped.

"Don't go, not yet ... Aunt Rae." Sophie's fingers tightened around the doorknob.

Aunt Rae shook her head. "Alessandro wrote me a letter every day until ... there were no more. In one he wrote, *Life is change, my dearest Regina Rose. Life goes on. Catch hold and live it.*" Aunt Rae's voice brightened a little, like the first time she had talked about Alessandro. "Life certainly does go on, Sophie. Whether we want it to or not."

"May I ask something ... about Alessandro?"

Aunt Rae breathed a long breath in, then nodded.

"Did he know ... about me?"

Aunt Rae looked at Sophie. "I wrote him. But I never heard back."

"That stone in the cemetery? The one with his initials and the rose. You said he was buried in Italy."

"He is. We put a memorial stone in the orchard. A place for remembering."

Sophie walked over to her aunt. "When you go to that place in Italy, I would like to go with you."

Aunt Rae looked up at her daughter. "I've missed so much, Sophie."

A soft breeze blew in through the open window; the lace curtain uncurled, billowed out, then returned to its place.

Aunt Rae reached over to Sophie. She took Sophie's hands in her own, her piano-playing hands. Sophie could hear Nonna's words: *Breathe,* bambino, *and live. Your mother loves you.*

Your mother loves you.

Sophie looked at her aunt, this stranger she was seeing for the very first time. And then she looked at the piano keys.

"Please, Aunt Rae, play."

Sing to me.

Acknowledgments

With gratitude, *grazie mille!*

I thank Ellen Howard, who introduced me to the murky process of discovery and reminded me, *Focus!* My mentors at Vermont College of Fine Arts, thank you, especially Marc Aronson, Jane Kurtz, and Julie Larios, who said, *Yes, sing your words.* My Flagstaff Plateau Writers, gratitude to each of you for your encouragement and insights. Once again, Jane Resh Thomas and Carolyn Coman at their Whole Novel Retreat swung open cellar doors and hayloft windows, asking, *What is this story about, what do these characters want?*

Family was my answer. I thank my own family, Megan, Michael, Elizabeth, and Macey, for your belief in my dreams, and Bill, my lifetime companion, for countless walks and talks.

To each reader, our family's song, *Donna nobis pacem,* a song of hope, forgiveness, and peace.

And to Stephen Roxburgh, editor *magnifico,* again, *grazie mille!*

—Nancy Bo Flood

Made in the USA
Middletown, DE
03 December 2019